WILEY & GRAMPA'S CREATURE FEATURES

JURASSIC GRAMPA

WRITTEN AND ILLUSTRATED BY

KIRK SCROGGS

CLASH OF THE OLD LIZARDS!

LITTLE, BROWN AND COMPANY
Books for Young Readers
New York   Boston

Special thanks to:
Steve Deline, Jackie Greed, Mark Mayes, Hiland Hall, Alejandra,
Inge Govaerts, Suppasak Viboonlarp, Joe Kocian, Christa, Jim Jeong,
Cindy Schmidt, and Will Keightly.

Andrea, Jill, Ames, Elizabeth, Saho, Maria, and the Little Brown Crew- woo woo!

Virginia Grumbles, Jeanne Moran, and Martha Brennan.

A scaly, gargantuan thanks to Ashley & Carolyn Grayson, Dav Pilkey,
Andrea, and the Mrs. Nelson's Books crew.

And an ancient prehistoric, fire-breathing thanks to Mamacita,
Corey and Candace, and Harold Aulds.

Little, Brown Books for Young Readers

Hachette Book Group
237 Park Avenue, New York, NY 10017
Visit our Web site at www.lb-kids.com

Little, Brown Books for Young Readers is a division of Hachette Book Group, Inc.
The Little, Brown name and logo are trademarks of Hachette Book Group, Inc.

First Edition: January 2009

The characters and events portrayed in this book are fictitious. Any similarity to real persons, living or
dead, is coincidental and not intended by the author.

ISBN: 978-0-316-00692-7

10 9 8 7 6 5 4 3 2 1

CW

Printed in the United States of America

Series design by Saho Fujii

The illustrations for this book were done in Staedtler ink on Canson Marker paper,
then digitized with Adobe Photoshop for color and shade.
The text was set in Humana Sans Light and the display type was handlettered.

CHAPTERS

CHAPTER 1

Hey, Lizard Breath!

Ladies and gentlemen, paleontologists, archeologists, and any other "ologist" out there . . .
The Earth's crust is made up of many layers.
The top layer is rich in nutrients, minerals, and juicy earthworms. Under that is a layer of volcanic rock millions of years old. Beneath that is a layer of fluffy, delicious cherry marshmallow filling, and beneath that you'll find . . .

A terrifying dinosaur the size of a turnip truck!

Wait a minute! That's just a cute little lizard my best friend, Jubal, and I discovered out in the desert.

"Hey, little lady," I said.

"Let's name her Lupe," said Jubal, "after my crazy great-aunt from El Paso."

You see, we were riding through the Saddlesore Mountains on horseback with my Grampa, Gramma, and Merle, the cat. We were in search of buried treasure, dinosaur bones, and rugged adventure.

"Actually, I'd rather search for a Slurpee or maybe an air-conditioned ice cream parlor," said Grampa.

CHAPTER 2

Spelunkin' Donuts

Lupe the lizard guided us to an old abandoned aluminum foil mine called Nostril Caverns.

"This place looks strangely familiar," said Grampa. "I feel like I've been here before, but I can't quite put my finger on it."

We made our way through the caverns. It was dark, dank, dangerous, and drippy.

We climbed over stalagmites, which point up, ducked under stalactites, which point down, and climbed a rock shaped like Grampa, which was pretty pointless.

CAVE TURKEY

MINERS MUST BE ACCOMPANIED BY A PARENT OR GUARDIAN

"Stay close to me, people!" said Grampa. "Pay no mind to that crunching sound beneath your feet. It's just thousands of albino cave beetles. And don't worry — they don't eat people. They feed on the guano from the millions of blood-sucking bats that are suspended above us. Now let's enjoy the rest of our hike."

"Look!" I shouted. "There's a complete bronto-saurus skeleton embedded in that rock. This is the discovery of a lifetime!"

"What would happen if I tugged on this?" asked Grampa as he jiggled a leg bone that was sticking out of the rock.

"Noooo!" I yelled. "Stop pulling his leg!"

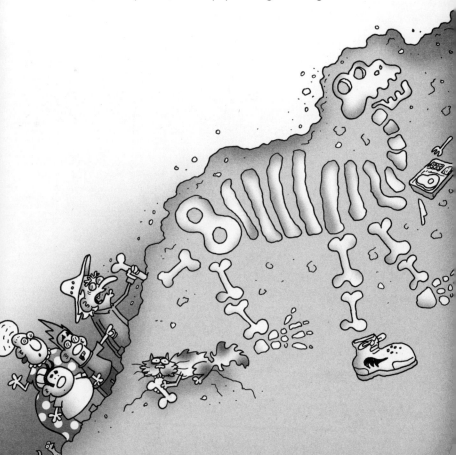

But it was too late.

Grampa dislodged the bone, which started a
terrifying chain reaction. The ground rumbled.
Jubal's belly quivered like a bowl of lime Jell-O.
Then a giant, petrified dinosaur egg came
tumbling toward us!

We tried to run, but the natural bridge we'd come in on had collapsed.

"This is it!" said Grampa. "Flattened by a giant egg. We're gonna look like a five-cheese and lizard omelet!"

"I don't think so!" screamed Gramma as she lassoed a stalactite above us with her long hair.

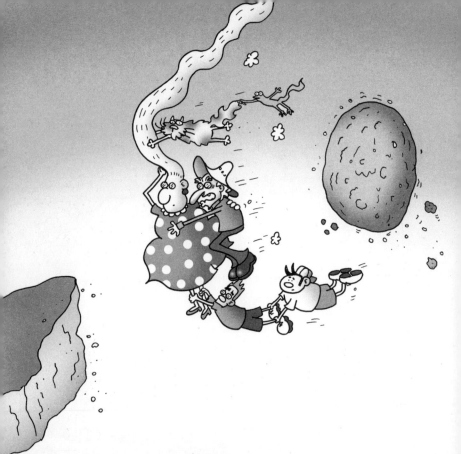

We all jumped onto Gramma and swung across the ravine Tarzan-style just in time.

"We've been married sixty years and I still haven't figured out that hair of yours!" said Grampa.

At last, we spilled out of the caverns in a heap, and boy was it good to be back on safe ground. But someone was waiting for us.

"Vell, vell, vell," said a voice. "Vhat do ve have here?"

"I recognize that voice," Grampa said. "From the sound of all those 'V' words, it could only be —"

Hans Lotion and his grandson, Jurgen. Gingham County's most notorious criminals, wanted for kidnapping, possession of a deadly crawdad, and coughing without covering their mouths.

"I believe you have found somezing rare and expensive," said Hans. "Hand it over!"

"Do what he says, Wiley," said Grampa. "They're armed with cake mixers."

"You can't have our dino egg!" I shouted. "We found it fair and square!"

"Dino egg? Hah!" said Hans. "Zat is no egg. It is somezing even more valuable — petrified dino dooky!"

"Dooky?" said Grampa. "Does anyone have any hand sanitizer?"

Hans and Jurgen rolled the petrified poop into the back of their truck and took off.

"Sayonara, suckers!" said Hans as they drove away. "Have a nice day! Hee! Hee!"

"I've decided that I really don't like those guys," said Jubal.

CHAPTER 3

The Morning Blues

Our story was big news. Grampa was even interviewed by Channel 5's Blue Norther.

"It was horrible," said Grampa. "We struggled and strained for that dooky, then it was swiped right out from under us. All that hard work flushed down the drain. It really stinks!"

"Don't worry," said Blue. "We'll get to the bottom of this and get that dooky back in your hands, where it belongs."

After watching Grampa on the news, we had a delicious breakfast loaded with bacon, eggs, extra-strong coffee for Merle, and hotcakes. But poor Grampa had to eat healthy whole-grain cereal.

"The doctor says I have to eat more fiber," said Grampa, "so your Gramma's been feeding me pebbles and dry twigs. She won't even let me eat my beloved Pork Cracklins. I think you should report her to the authorities."

Suddenly, the alarm on Gramma's new watch went off.

"Ooh! It's time to take your laxative," said Gramma, shoving a heaping spoonful of milky blue liquid into Grampa's mouth. "The doctor said to take it every six hours."

"I can hardly wait for the next delicious dose," said Grampa.

CHAPTER 4

Project Runaway!

Later that day at school, Lupe the lizard was a huge hit in science class. Ms. Frecklebeak, our teacher, even let everyone stop work on their science projects to gather around America's most talented reptile.

Lupe could stand on her hind feet like a meerkat.

She could beat anyone in a staring competition, even Harvey Blinkless, who was born without eyelids.

And her skateboarding skills were sick. (That's skateboarder speak for "pretty cool.")

Ms. Frecklebeak was most impressed. "Gentlemen, I nominate this lizard to be our new class
mascot, replacing Gertie, the guinea pig who is
oh-so-yesterday's news. Pack your bags, Gertie!"

She rewarded Lupe with a snack of Nature's
Nuggets all-organic lizard pellets with actual
bits of dried dragonflies. Yum!

Then something strange happened. Lupe started to gyrate and jerk uncontrollably!

"Look!" said the Sugar Sisters. "That lizard's 'bout to bust a move!"

Lupe started to grow, and she sprouted huge, razor-sharp teeth that were dripping with dragonfly bits.

Before long, Lupe had transformed into a full-size T. rex! And she was no longer so sweet.

"Could somebody shoo this lizard out the door?" said Ms. Frecklebeak. "And tell Gertie the guinea pig she's my favorite again!"

We quickly reported to our battle stations and unleashed the fury of the most dangerous weapons on Earth — our science projects.

I let Lupe have it with my vinegar and baking soda volcano.

Jubal launched a tumbling tater from his hand-crafted potato launcher.

The Sugar Sisters washed out the lizard's mouth with their disgusting homemade lard soap.

And little Ronty Derlick fired his Watermelon Conversion Laser Blaster that can turn any melon or medium-sized pork roast into a laser beam.

"What a show-off," said Jubal.

But the melon-scented laser beams only made Lupe angrier, and she chased us out into the hall.

"Run, fellow students!" I screamed. "There's a T. rex on the loose, and she's having some serious anger-management issues!"

Vera the lunch lady tried to appease the T. rex with a healthy portion of her world-famous Salisbury steak with candied hog snouts. Lupe screeched in horror!

"Wow!" said Jubal. "Even vicious carnivores are terrified by Salisbury steak."

Lupe fled from the cursed cuisine and burst through the wall.

"Look!" I screamed. "The T. rex is running straight for the preschool and the old folks' home!"

"Thank goodness!" said Ms. Frecklebeak. "At least it's someone else's problem now."

CHAPTER 5

Iguana Be Sedated

Suddenly, a humongous military vehicle pulled
up and two women dressed in safari gear
jumped out.

"Stand back, people!" said one of the women,
twirling a lasso. "Ladies with live ammo and
large hair comin' through!"

The bigger woman lassoed the T. rex's foot to trip it up.

The smaller lady jumped on the T. rex's back and zapped it with a 400,000-volt stun gun, which is the proper voltage for a T. rex but too much for a small rodent or a little brother.

Then they fitted the beast with a shiny electric collar that calmed it down.

And finished off with a pedicure and a fresh coat of sparkleberry nail polish.

"It's all under control, little darlin's!" said the large woman. "I'm Winona Pellet, and this is my sister, Petunia, owners of Nature's Nuggets all-organic pet food. We grow all the ingredients and brew our own rich, meaty gravy."

"She's making me hungry," said Jubal.

"We'll take this big ol' lizard to our compound for further study," said Winona.

The Pellet Sisters strapped Lupe to the top of their SUV and took off for their giganto Nature's Nuggets compound.

"I hope they take care of Lupe," said Jubal. "Even though she tried to devour us, I still have a soft spot for her."

"There's something familiar about those two," I said. "I don't trust 'em."

CHAPTER 6

After-school Spectacular

I couldn't wait to tell Grampa about our crazy
school day. I invited Jubal over and we hopped
off the school bus to find . . .

All heck was breaking loose! Grampa was up in
a tree, being poked and prodded by two woolly
mammoths!

"Helllllp!" yelped Grampa. "I'm being attacked
by Mister Snuffyluffagus and his slightly hairier
sister!"

I pulled Grampa out of the tree while Jubal distracted the mammoths with some peanut butter and Gummi Bear sandwiches he had in his pocket.

"Hey!" said Grampa as I dragged him to safety. "Throw one of those sandwiches this way, will ya? All I've eaten today is a bowl of twigs."

Once inside, we barricaded the door. Grampa was babbling incoherently.

"Snap out of it!" I said, slapping him upside the head. "Now tell us. What happened?"

"One minute I'm feeding Esther and Chavez some puppy pellets; the next, they turn into angry mastodons and chase me up a tree. I haven't seen anything as horrifyingly hairy since your uncle Artie wore that pair of Speedos."

CHAPTER 7

Fish Out of Water!

Grampa was cut short by a scream from Gramma, who was battling a megalodon that was bursting out of Paco's fishbowl!

"I don't know what happened!" said Gramma. "This morning Paco seemed normal, then, after lunch, he transformed into a fifty-ton species of the genus Carcharodon, thought to have been extinct since the Pliocene era more than 1.5 million years ago!"

I managed to jam Paco's mouth with a vacuum cleaner, but he was growing bigger and bigger by the second.

"Why would perfectly normal hound dogs turn into mammoths and a cute goldfish go great white on us?" I asked.

All of a sudden, we heard a roar from the living room.

We looked over to see Merle by his cat bowl,
only Merle wasn't himself. He had turned into
a prehistoric saber-toothed house cat and was
staring at us like we were filet mignon with
chicken giblet gravy!

"Merle, you look different," said Grampa. "Have
you been working out?"

Merle jumped right at us with his huge, slobbery fangs. But instead of clawing us, he jumped past us to his scratching post and started purring.

"Still the same ol' Merle," said Grampa.

CHAPTER 8

A Battle of Mammoth Proportions

We grabbed Merle and took off across the yard
for Grampa's car. The mammoths were in hot
pursuit.

"Look!" screamed Gramma. "The chickens have transformed into pterodactyls and one is flying off with the car!"

"Well, it's been that kind of day," said Grampa.

CHAPTER 9

Tykes on Trikes

"Hey, you!" screamed a small child with a snotty nose and a whole posse of kids on Big Wheelz trikes. "Prehistoric hairy butts!"

"Don't talk about my family that way," said Grampa.

"Not you!" screamed the tyke. "I'm talkin' to the moronic mammoths and the birdbrained flying lizards. Pick on someone your own size!"

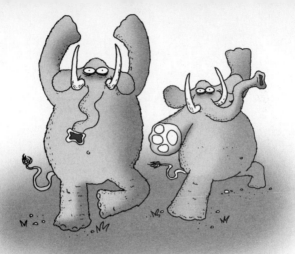

Dem was fightin' words. Esther and Chavez
struck their Drunken Mammoth Monkey
stance.

But two of the biker kids snuck in from behind
and tripped the beasts with their Big Wheelin'
Bamboo Maneuver.

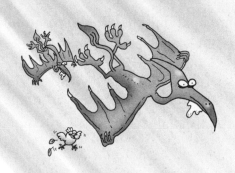

The pterodactyl chickens dive-bombed in a screaming eagle formation.

But the head biker spun out on his trike and sent a wave of pebbles and dirt into their eyes, which really irritated their contact lenses.

Grampa, Gramma, and Jubal hitched rides with the bikers, while I rode Merle kittyback-style.

"Put the pedal to the plastic!" yelled Grampa. "They're gaining on us!"

"The whole town's gone prehistoric," said the head biker. "All the pets have turned on us! My own canary tried to eat my left pinky toe just this morning."

"I hate to tell you this," I said, "but you've got a glob of mucus hanging from your nose."

"That's how we roll, daddy-o!" said a biker with glasses. "We're known as the Snot-Nosed Punks. We wear it like a badge of honor. It's way cool."

"Hey, look!" said Grampa, pointing at his nose. "I'm cool, too."

CHAPTER 10

Wild in the Streets

"We'll drop you off in town, where you'll be safe," said the punk. "We've gotta get back home for apple juice and nap time."

Downtown Gingham was nuts. Dinosaurs ran amok while the Pellet Sisters were busy trying to wrangle them into their vehicle. But there were just too many monsters.

"My parakeet turned into a pteranodon," said Old Man Jorgensen. "I wouldn't stand underneath him if I were you!"

"I can't even keep up with my Seeing Eye raptor!" said Jack Moss, a local banker.

"My doggy turned into a *Torvosaurus*!" said little Carol Diane. "Boy! They do not like bubble baths!"

Nate Farkles's veterinarian's office was a shambles, too. Everyone and their dog — er, dinosaur — had shown up wanting answers.

"I don't know what to tell you," said Nate. "Every pet in Gingham has devolved into a primitive beast. It's making my job very difficult. Have you ever tried to give a velociraptor a rabies shot? It's no picnic."

"Ooooh!" yelped Gramma. "Some little critter's got hold of my patooty!"

"Fascinating," said Nate. "Moments ago, this was just a simple hamster. Now it is a new species of dinosaur. We shall have to come up with a name for it."

"How about an *Omybunsarsaurus*?" said Grampa.

"Something just dawned on me," I said. "Lupe, Esther and Chavez, and Paco all ate Nature's Nuggets pet food before they transformed."

"And I fed Merle Nature's Nuggets Kitty Pellets with peppercorn sauce and a glass of sparkling apple juice, slightly chilled," said Gramma.

"If my hunch is correct," I said, "this food is turning our prized pets into primal predators."

"Then I probably shouldn't be eating this doggy biscuit," said Grampa, munching away.

"No, Grampa!" I screamed. "You don't know what that could do to you!"

"That's right!" said Gramma. "The doctor said you shouldn't be eating any cookies!"

CHAPTER 11

Are You Smarter Than a Five-Million-Year-Old?

Suddenly, Grampa started to convulse and clutch his belly.

"Egads!" said Grampa. "I haven't felt this bad since I ate that expired carton of tapioca pudding!"

Then he began to mutate and burst right through his clothes!

"Grampa's turned into a caveman!" I said. "I shall call him *Neandernumbskull.*"

"Your feeble attempts at humor are immature," snarled Grampa.

"Wow! Check out those big words," said Jubal. "Caveman Grampa is actually smarter than regular Grampa."

"A most astute observation, young man," said Grampa. "Bravo!"

"Hey! Take a look at this," Nate said, pointing at his microscope.

"Gross!" I said. "I see a pulsating clump of mush and hair. This must be the pet food's secret ingredient!"

"Actually, it's just a sample of my earwax," said Nate. "I always wanted to see what it looked like up close."

"We have to get inside that pet food plant to investigate," I said. "But how?"

"Elementary, my dear Wiley," said caveman Grampa. "We shall disguise ourselves, infiltrate their diabolical compound, and incarcerate the villainous vermin at once!"

"I have no idea what any of those words mean, but I love it!" I said. "Nate, if we're not back in three hours, send for help."

"Affirmative!" said Nate.

CHAPTER 12

Disguise the Limit

We put together an extremely convincing dinosaur costume and snuck our way up to the Pellet Sisters' pet-food fortress. A line of creatures was waiting to get in.

X-RAY VIEW

Grampa and Merle got in no problem, but the
Pellet Sisters stopped me and Jubal and Gramma
in our brontosaurus outfit.

"What a pitiful specimen," said Winona Pellet.
"Just look at its scraggly hide, poor posture,
and that enormous butt! I shall call you
Sadsackasaurus. Get in there and hit the gym."

I could feel Gramma's anger meter heating up.

Once inside the compound, we broke off from the main group.

Then Grampa used Merle's saber teeth to pry open the door to the secret laboratory.

TOP
SECRET

EVIL
PERSONNEL
ONLY!

CHAPTER 13

Yabba Dabba Dooky!

We ditched the costume and explored the spooky lab.

We found hundreds of grotesque specimens and electronic gadgets.

"Look!" I said. "It's the stolen dino dooky! That must be the secret ingredient in the pet food! The last time we saw that cursed poop, it was in the hands of—"

"You mean **Hans**!" It was Hans Lotion and his
grandson, Jurgen, and they were holding up
their Pellet Sisters masks. "Ve're baaaack! Hold
your applause, please. It feels good to get out of
zese masks. You have no idea how hard it is to
vear vomen's clothes and pronounce your W's
correctly."

"Why on earth would you want to put dino poop in the pet food supply?" I asked.

"Not only does ze dooky give ze pet food a nutty, robust flavor," said Hans, "but it transforms ze creatures zat eat it into zere prehistoric ancestors. Dinosaurs, saber-toothed prairie dogs—you name it! And now I vill show you ze most amazing development in entertainment since ze piñata!"

CHAPTER 14

Pirates of the Reptilian

Hans took us on a scenic boat tour of his evil empire.

"Velcome to my extreme sports facility," said Hans. "Here ve train ze prehistoric beasts to be ze best of ze best. No vimps allowed!"

"Over zere, ve see some ultimate, no-holds-barred raptor kickboxing."

"And zere, ve have my beautiful tyrannosaurs training for ze Dino-Bowl."

"Here, ve see two beasts engaged in a battle of
extreme checkers."

"And here, I have a deadly pile-driving
Ankylosaurus."

"You should put some ice on that," said Gramma.

Zat's Entertainment!

"And zis is your last stop," said Hans, jumping off the boat into a huge coliseum packed with spectators, "Ze Dino Dome! Vhere mere humans are forced to battle carnivorous creatures for my enjoyment. Order it now for only $12.95 on Pay per Viewed."

"One more zing!" said Hans, arming us with foam rubber weapons. "You are ze first contestants. Prepare for battle and just have fun vith it!"

"This is an outrage!" I said. "Surely the crowd won't allow us to become a five-course dino dinner."

But boy was I wrong. The crowd was made up of master criminals . . .

Like Rocco Stenchberger, crime lord over the dangerous world of black-market tube socks.

The Skink family. Known for gambling, talking during movies, and plucking the wings off butterflies.

And Dr. Marcus Vein Brain, one-hundred-year-old inventor of black licorice and creamed spinach.

Grampa, Jubal, and I were thrown into the arena
and pitted against our old pal, Lupe the T. rex.

"Don't vorry, folks!" said Hans. "Ze T. rex has
been fitted vith a protective helmet and flame-
thrower just to make sure it's a fair fight."

"How thoughtful," said Jubal.

Gramma and Merle were sent to the world's
lousiest swimming pool, where they had to face
off against Paco the megalodon.

"Paco!" said Gramma. "Don't you recognize me?
Remember how I used to feed you dried gnats and
then we'd go synchronized swimming together?"

Lupe chased us up a massive obstacle course.

"Grampa," I said, "this might be a good time for you to go caveman crazy and fight back."

"My dear Wiley," said Grampa. "Violence is not the answer. I shan't sink to that lizard's level."

"Boy," said Jubal. "Caveman Grampa is so disappointing."

"I think I know how to get his goat," I said. "Hey, Grampa! Did you know that Hans has secret plans to destroy all known stockpiles of Pork Cracklins and outlaw them forever?"

"No Pork Cracklins?!!" bellowed Grampa. "Forever?!! That make Caveman Grampa upset! Caveman Grampa angry! Caveman Grampa go crazy!!!"

HAVING FUN YET?

And go crazy he did. Grampa batted away raptors and pterodactyls like fruit flies.

Then he swung Lupe around by the tail like a sack of dirty laundry.

CHAPTER 16

Time to Go

Suddenly, Gramma's watch went off again.

"Ooh!" she said. "It's time for your laxative!"

Gramma reached up and pulled the bottle of Mighty Lax out of her big hair.

Then she tossed it to Grampa, who chugged the milky blue liquid like a refreshing beverage.

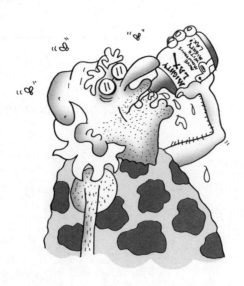

Mighty Lax works extremely fast, and Grampa needed a bathroom quick!

"Ladies and gentlemen!" said Hans. "Ve vill now pause for a brief potty break. After Grampa-pa uses ze johnny, ve vill return to ze violent man-eating action already in progress."

The porta-potty lurched and shook and Grampa let out a long groan and a shriek—all the normal stuff that happens when Grampa uses the bathroom.

But when Grampa came out, he was back to his old self!

"I feel good. I feel fresh," said Grampa, "but I wouldn't go in there for at least ten minutes, if you know what I mean."

CHAPTER 17

What a Potty Mouth

"The Mighty Lax must have driven out the effects of the dino dooky!" I said. "Let's test it on Lupe!"

Just as she attacked, I lovingly dripped just one drop on Lupe's tongue. She started to tremble and looked anxious.

Lupe politely excused herself and went behind a crate to do her business and some light reading.

Within seconds, Lupe was just a little ol' lizard again.

"It sure is nice not having to worry about her clawing our eyes out anymore," said Grampa.

Gramma then gave Paco a drop.

Merle slipped some to the pterodactyls.

And he even took a swig for himself.

CHAPTER 18

In the Line of Doody

Pretty soon, the line to the little dinosaurs' room stretched all the way down the hall, and the dinos were coming out refreshed and back to their normal, non-man-eating selves.

"How do you like that, Hans?" I yelled. "Your plan is poo-poo! No one's gonna pay $12.95 to see humans battling house cats, chickens, and hamsters."

"You may be right, Viley!" said Hans. "But I bet zey vould pay big bucks to see a giant robot-turkey squash you like an overripe vatermelon!"

"Could you repeat that last part?" said Grampa.

Hans' podium rose up out of the stands and transformed into a giant robot-bird loaded with missiles, cannons, and spinning blades.

"I vould like you to meet *Robo Turkeysaurus*," said Hans. "Ze latest in lethal, fuel-efficient, metal turkey technology."

"First, I vill show you my flame-broiling skills," said Hans as he hosed us down with fire from his built-in flame-thrower.

"Zen, I vill demonstrate my carving technique vith my rotating Dino Saw!"

"And no meal vould be complete vithout some mashed spuds!"

"And some home-style hydrochloric acid gravy!"

"The meal he's describing just doesn't sound appetizing," said Jubal.

All of a sudden we heard a loud roar and a stomp behind us. It was Gramma, except she was green, fifty feet tall, and twenty tons!

"Gramma must have eaten one of those dog biscuits so she could become a dinosaur and take on the *Turkeysaurus*," I said.

"Either that or she needs to go on a serious diet!" said Grampa.

GRAMMA'S ANGER METER
(CURRENTLY THE TEMPERATURE OF MOLTEN MAGMA)

CHAPTER 19

Cold Turkey

In the first round, Gramma knocked the stuffing out of that jive turkey!

Then she practiced a move she learned on WWE — the dreaded Poultry Tenderizer!

Then came a vicious round of Patty-Cake!

"Don't look, Wiley. This may not be pretty. When Gramma plays Patty-Cake, someone usually loses an arm."

The *Robo Turkeysaurus* was in bad shape. He was missing a leg, leaking vital fluids, and his cholesterol levels were way too high.

"You've von zis round," said Hans, "but I have a backup plan. In twenty seconds I launch my Rumproaster Missile. You'll all be blown into crispy turkey nuggets. Hee! Hee!"

"I hate his backup plans," said Jubal.

CHAPTER 20

Snot Over 'Til It's Over

Suddenly, Nate Farkles and the Snot-Nosed Punks burst in through the wall!

"Freeze, master criminals!" said the head punk.

"You guys said to get help if I didn't hear from you," said Nate. "So I brought a bunch of four-year-olds. They're all I could find."

"Listen up, punks!" I screamed. "We only have twenty seconds until Hans launches a—"

"No! You listen up, old man!" said the head punk. "You get these civilians out of here, contact the authorities, and leave that half-turkey/half-dishwasher to us! Got it?"

"Uh . . .," I said. "Okay."

"Okay what?" demanded the punk.

"Okay . . . sir?" I said.

Man, these punks were bossy.

While we evacuated
the building, the punks
climbed up the turkey's
leg like a jungle gym.

But it was too late! The *Robo Turkeysaurus* launched the killer missile and it zoomed out at us. But then something odd happened. The missile was stuck to the turkey with a rubbery substance that looked like green bubble gum. It stretched the green goo to the breaking point, then the missile just stopped in mid-air.

"Go avay, missile!" said Hans nervously. "Fly avay and be free!"

But the missile blew up in the most massive explosion since The Great Microwave Popcorn Disaster of 1984! We ran for our lives in a shower of shrapnel and turkey leftovers.

"Don't cry for me, Gingham County!" shouted Hans, who had hitched a ride on a pterodactyl chicken. "Ve'll be back! And next time ve'll have an army of bigger, better metal turkeys and bring zis town to its knees! Or, maybe ve could just do dinner or play Parcheesi or somezing. Just give me a call."

Even though Hans and Jurgen had escaped and
Gramma was the size of a 747, things seemed
back to normal.

"I'm impressed by you punks," I said. "But where
did you get all that green bubble gum to put on
that missile?"

"Who said it was bubble gum?" said the head
punk, his nose looking surprisingly clean.

So, that's my story. The police had a heck of a time getting all those master criminals into their squad car.

We used Mighty Lax to make the rest of the dinosaurs regular again, and Gramma and Grampa even starred in one of the company's commercials.

Nostril Caverns was plugged up, and all the remaining dino dooky and Nature's Nuggets pet food was destroyed.

Except for two doggy biscuits.

"Jubal, we must destroy these samples," I said. "Most kids would do anything to be able to turn into a prehistoric monster. But not us. Oh no! There is no way we will eat these doggy biscuits ..."

Boy, were we gonna be in big trouble.

CRACKPOT SNAPSHOT

WANTED

HANS LOTION AND HIS GRANDSON, JURGEN

Gingham County Police have printed up "Wanted" posters for criminal masterminds Hans Lotion and his grandson, Jurgen. Something about that second poster seems a little wacky. Help us find the differences before we send them to *America's Most Haunted*.

The answers are on the next page. Anyone caught cheating has to give Hans' pet velociraptor, Snookybuns, a Swedish back rub.